# My FURRY FOSTER FAMILY

# Apple and Annie, the Hamster Duo

written by Debbi Michiko Florence

illustrated by Melanie Demmer

raintree

a Capstone company — publishers for children

To my aunt, Toshie Hatami, the best hamster mum! – DMF

Raintree is an imprint of Capstone Global Library Limited, a company incorporated in England and Wales having its registered office at 264 Banbury Road, Oxford, OX2 7DY – Registered company number: 6695582

www.raintree.co.uk
myorders@raintree.co.uk

Designed by Lori Bye
Original illustrations © Capstone Global Library Limited 2020
Originated by Capstone Global Library Ltd

978 1 4747 8495 5

**British Library Cataloguing in Publication Data**
A full catalogue record for this book is available from the British Library.

**Acknowledgements**
We would like to thank the following for ~~~~ ~~~~ ~~~~ ~~~~ ~~~~ ~~~~
Melanie Demmer, 71; Roy Thomas, 70

Every effort has been made to contact ~~~~ ~~~~ ~~~~ ~~~~ ~~~~
omissions will be rectified in subsequen~~~~

Printed and bound in India

# Contents

Dad
(Tim Takano)

Mum
(Cindy Takano)

Me
(Kaita Takano)

Eraser

Ollie

Joss Lawrence,
Happy Tails
Rescue

Hannah Miller,
my best friend

# CHAPTER 1

# The long wait

I love lots of things. I love my family, my dog and my best friend, Hannah, most of all. When we're all together, I am a very happy girl.

Last Tuesday, Hannah came home with me and my mum after school. Ollie, my mini dachshund, greeted us loudly when we walked in the kitchen door. *Yip! Yip! Yip!*

Mum opened the fridge and asked, "Girls, how about a snack?"

"No, thank you, Mrs Takano," Hannah said.

I smiled. I was pleased to hear that. Hannah and I had plans. It was a special day. I didn't want to waste time eating snacks, even though I really like snack time!

"I bet Ollie would like a snack," Hannah said. "Can I give him one?"

"Of course!" Mum said.

Hannah reached into a jar on the worktop. Ollie wagged his tail. He knew what was in that jar.

"Ollie, sit!" Hannah said. She held up a dog biscuit.

Ollie sat.

"Good boy!" Hannah said. She
threw the treat, and Ollie caught
it in mid-air.

Hannah and I went into the living room. We sat on the sofa and looked out of the window. We were waiting for a special visitor.

"What time is Joss coming?" Hannah asked.

"I don't know," I said, bouncing on the sofa. "I can't wait to see the new pets she's bringing. They're going to be so sweet!"

Joss is a woman who works for Happy Tails Rescue. It's a wonderful place that helps homeless animals. Last year my family adopted Ollie from Happy Tails. Now we foster pets for them. That means we take care of animals until they find a forever home.

"What are you getting this time?" Hannah asked. "A bird? Perhaps more kittens?"

I shook my head. "Two dwarf hamsters! They're sisters!" I said.

"Hamsters!" Hannah squealed. "Amazing!"

Sometimes Hannah comes to the pet shop with me to buy Ollie's dog food. We always stop to look at the animals, especially the furry ones. We like watching the hamsters. They look so cute, running on their exercise wheels.

"Do you know how to take care of hamsters?" Hannah asked. "They're probably going to be very different from Ollie."

I nodded. "Mum found a book about hamsters for me at the bookshop," I said. "It's so great she works there. I've read the book three times already."

Hannah and I looked out of the window again. I hoped Joss' van would pull into the driveway soon. Waiting was hard.

I stroked Ollie. Hannah stroked Ollie. Then Ollie fell asleep.

"You are so lucky to have a dog," Hannah said.

"You can play with Ollie whenever you want," I said.

"Thank you, Kaita," Hannah said with a smile.

I looked out of the window yet again.

Mum walked into the living room. She wore her straw hat. She always wore it when she worked in the garden. "Are you girls just sitting here, looking out of the window?" she asked.

"We're waiting for Joss," I said.

"You can help in the garden, if you'd like," Mum said. "How about working on a puzzle? Time will seem to go faster."

"A puzzle would be good. It *is* a bit boring to wait," Hannah said. She gave a little smile and patted my shoulder. "Sorry, Kaita."

"That's OK," I said. "I'm a bit bored, too."

I grabbed a puzzle box off the shelf. Hannah and I sat on the floor by the coffee table and poured out the pieces. The puzzle was a picture of ocean animals. Brightly coloured fish, a sea turtle and a dolphin swam in the water.

Hannah and I picked through the pile. We looked for edge pieces first. Then we slowly started to put the edge pieces together. I love the happy clicking sound puzzle pieces make when they fit together! Soon we had finished the entire edge.

Without warning Ollie woke up and ran to the front door. *Yip! Yip! Yip!*

"Joss is here!" Mum said, coming in from the garden.

I looked at the clock. An hour had flown by! Mum was right. Doing the puzzle had kept us busy.

Mum picked up Ollie and opened the door.

"Hello, Takano family!" Joss said. "Hello, Hannah!"

Ollie wagged his tail and wiggled in Mum's arms.

"Yes, hello to you, too, Ollie!" Joss said.

Ollie liked Joss. A lot! Joss had fostered Ollie while he was waiting for his forever family – US!

Joss carried a big plastic container. It looked like one of the tubs Mum kept my old schoolwork in. This one was bigger, though, without a lid.

Our new foster animals had finally arrived!

I leaned in to look. Bubbles of excitement tickled my tummy.

Then the bubbles popped.

I couldn't see any hamsters inside the plastic tub. Where were they?

# CHAPTER 2

# Meet Apple and Annie

I looked at Joss. "Have you forgetton the hamsters?" I asked. I hoped she hadn't. I didn't want to wait any longer!

"No, Kaita," Joss said with a smile. "Apple and Annie are in the little box inside this tub."

I looked again. I saw a box with air holes. I heard scratching sounds coming from inside it.

"We need to keep the hamsters in a room away from Ollie," Joss said. "I know he wouldn't hurt them on purpose, but it's better to keep the pets apart."

Mum led Joss to our guest room. It's a small room that my dad sometimes uses as his studio. Dad is a graphic artist. He makes things like adverts and logos. Sometimes Dad and I draw pictures together.

Joss put the tub on top of a table. "The hamsters won't be able to climb up the sides of the tub," she said. "To be safe, though, always keep the door to this room closed."

"Cool," I said, looking closely inside. "It looks like a mini playground."

"It does!" Hannah said, peering over my shoulder.

In the middle of the tub was a red exercise wheel. A yellow plastic tube lay beside it. The hamsters could run on the wheel and race through the tube. I wished I was a hamster so I could play in there!

The tub also held a water bottle and a green dish full of seeds. Litter covered the bottom of the tub. It looked like tiny balls of brown paper.

"Ready to meet Apple and Annie?" Joss asked.

"Ready!" Hannah and I said.

Joss opened the box. Out climbed two furry, tan-and-white hamsters.

"Cute!" I said. I smiled so wide my

cheeks hurt.

"Apple and Annie lived together with a nice family. Sadly one of the children was allergic to them. Whenever he was near the hamsters, he sneezed and coughed. So now Apple and Annie need a new home."

"Which one is which?" Hannah asked. The hamsters looked the same.

Joss pointed to one of them. "See that spot that looks like a crooked apple? That's Apple!" she said.

"Can I hold her?" I asked.

"Yes, of course," Joss said. "In fact, I hope you will play with both hamsters a lot. They get used to being touched, and that makes them better pets."

Joss scooped up Apple and put her in my hands. I giggled.

"She's so soft," I said.

I cupped my hands so Apple wouldn't get away. Then I lifted her to my face. We were nose to nose. Apple wiggled her whiskers. She was adorable!

"Would you like to hold Annie?" Joss asked Hannah.

Hannah nodded, and Joss put Annie in her hands. Now each of us had a hamster to play with.

After a few minutes, Joss wished us luck and said goodbye. Apple started to crawl up my arm. Annie squirmed in Hannah's hands. The hamsters' little feet tickled. I didn't want our new foster pets to escape, so Hannah and I put them back in the tub.

We watched the hamsters play for a while. Apple ran on the exercise wheel. Annie stuffed seeds into her mouth. Her cheeks puffed out like balloons. Hannah and I laughed.

When Apple got off the wheel, she ran through the tunnel a few times. So did Annie. Then they made a nest with the litter. They curled up next to each other and fell asleep.

"They don't play for very long," Hannah said. "Do you think they're bored? Like we were, waiting for Joss?"

"I'm not sure," I said. "Mum said hamsters are nocturnal. They sleep a lot during the day and move around at night. I think that's why Mum and Dad put them here in the guest room. They didn't want the hamsters to keep us awake while we were trying to sleep."

"OK. So maybe they *aren't* bored," Hannah said.

"Maybe they aren't," I said. I looked at the wheel and the tunnel. I knew what it felt like to not have enough fun things to do. "I have an idea. Come on! Let's go to my room!"

# CHAPTER 3

# Time for toys

Hannah and I sat down on my bedroom floor. Ollie came running in, wagging his tail.

"Did you miss us, Ollie?" I asked. I gave him a big hug. Hannah rubbed his muzzle. "I'm sorry you couldn't meet Apple and Annie. I think you'd make a good big brother!"

"So what's your idea, Kaita?" Hannah asked me.

"Let's make toys for Apple and Annie," I said.

Hannah smiled. "Yes! That sounds like fun!" she said.

I grabbed the hamster book Mum had got for me. Then I dragged out my art supply box from the cupboard. Ollie stuck his head in the box. He pulled out a cardboard tube and started chewing it.

"This book has some good projects in it," I said. "I've marked the best ones."

We flipped through the book and quickly got to work. Hannah made a house out of a square box. She cut out a door and windows. She called it the Hamster Hut.

I took two empty toilet-paper rolls and cut them in half. I taped the four short tubes to a piece of cardboard. "Look, Hannah," I said. "I've made a stage for them to climb on."

"Great!" she said.

With the leftover cardboard, we made a ramp.

When we had finished making the toys, we checked Apple and Annie. They were awake!

"Hello, Apple! Hello, Annie!" I said. "Look! We've made you two some toys."

Hannah placed the house on one side of the tub. I put the stage on the other side and set up the ramp over the tunnel. Then Hannah and I sat back and watched.

Apple scurried to Hannah's Hamster Hut straight away. She peeked in one of the windows. After a few seconds, she went inside.

"She likes it!" Hannah said.

Annie climbed over the ramp, back and forth. Neither hamster seemed to see my stage. I felt a bit sad about that. How could I get Apple and Annie to play on it?

I ran to the kitchen. Mum was making dinner. "Can I please have a few slices of carrot?" I asked.

Mum raised an eyebrow. She wasn't sure what I needed the carrots for. She cut a few slices for me anyway.

"Thanks!" I called, running back to the guest room.

I put the carrots on top of the stage. Apple sniffed the air. Then she and Annie followed their noses to the stage. Apple put her front paws on the cardboard and stretched. With a hop she was on top! Annie hopped up, too! The hamsters nibbled their treats. They looked so sweet holding the carrots in their paws.

"Great idea, Kaita," Hannah said.

Apple and Annie looked very happy. Hannah and I watched them play with their new toys until Hannah's mum picked her up for dinner.

\*\*\*

*Yip! Yip! Yip!* Ollie ran to the back door. Dad was home from work.

"Dad! Come and meet Apple and Annie! They are so tiny and cute! Hurry!" I said. I grabbed his arm and pulled.

"Let me take my shoes off first, Kaita," Dad said with a laugh.

I pulled Dad towards the guest room. I talked non-stop the whole way to the hamsters' tub.

"Joss said to keep the door closed," I said. "She's worried Ollie might upset the hamsters. I think he'd be nice, though. Don't you? He's a good boy."

"Yes, he is," Dad said. He looked into the tub. "Wow, you were right. They *are* tiny and cute."

Apple was in the house Hannah had made. Annie was running on

the wheel.

"They came with the tunnel and wheel. Hannah and I made the other toys," I said proudly.

Dad nodded. "I'm sure Apple and Annie are grateful for the gifts," he said.

After dinner, Mum went to work. Dad and I finished the puzzle that Hannah and I had started. Ollie snored on the sofa.

"Well done!" Dad said as we looked at the ocean picture.

"You too, Dad," I said. "Is it OK if I play with Apple and Annie before bedtime? Joss said we should play with them a lot."

"Absolutely," he said.

I skipped to the guest room and looked in the tub. Apple was running on the wheel. *Squeak! Squeak! Squeak!* I peeked in the house but couldn't see Annie.

"Well, where–" I started to say.

I heard a small scratching sound nearby. I looked around.

Annie was on the table, outside of the tub!

"Annie, what are you doing out here?" I said, scooping her up. "How did you get out?"

I stroked Annie's head with my finger. I was glad I had come to check on the hamsters when I did.

Thankfully they were safe.

I put Annie back in the tub with her sister. They greeted each other with a nose kiss.

I wondered how Annie had got

out. The sides of the tub were tall and slippery.

I told myself it was probably a one-off thing. I was sure it wouldn't happen again.

"Good night, Apple. Good night, Annie. I'm really glad you're here," I said. I turned out the light and went to my room.

# CHAPTER 4

# The great escape

The next morning I helped Dad make our special Saturday waffles. He cracked the eggs. I measured the flour, sugar and milk. I mixed. Then Dad scooped the batter into the waffle iron.

Breakfast was ready by the time Mum got back from her run. The waffles were delicious!

Mum went to work after breakfast. I cleaned Apple and Annie's tub. I gave them fresh seeds and water.

When I'd finished with the hamsters, Dad and I took Ollie to the dog park. Ollie got to play off his lead with the other dogs.

Our neighbour, Mrs Ahmed and her dog, Lucy, were already there. Lucy was a beagle. She and Ollie liked to chase each other.

"Hello, Kaita! Hello, Tim!" Mrs Ahmed said. "How are you today?"

"We're well, Mrs Ahmed!" I said.

"Are you still fostering all of those kittens?" she asked. "I think it's wonderful that you open your home to so many pets in need."

"No, all of the kittens found their forever families," I said. "We got two foster hamsters yesterday. Dwarf hamsters! They're sisters! They fit right in your hand. Would you like to adopt them?"

Mrs Ahmed smiled. "I don't think Lucy would like that very much, Kaita," she said. "I hope you find a good home for them."

"Thank you, Badia," Dad said. "I'm sure we will."

Mrs Ahmed got me thinking. I wondered what the perfect place for Apple and Annie would be. I asked Dad on the walk home.

"I talked to Joss about that," Dad said. "Hamsters need a house that's not too busy. They should get lots of playtime and attention. They're better pets for older children or adults. Little children don't always know how to be gentle. Hamsters are tiny, fragile animals, you know."

I nodded. "Holding a hamster is a bit like holding a soap bubble."

"That's right," Dad said.

"Apple and Annie need to be adopted together, too," I said. "It wouldn't be right to separate two sisters."

"Right again," Dad said. "They're a bonded pair. They need each other."

When we got home, Ollie took a long drink from his water bowl. I gave him a treat.

"Kaita, Mum will be home in an hour. What do you want to do until then?" Dad asked.

I didn't have to think for even a second about that.

"Play with Apple and Annie!" I said.

"OK," Dad said. "Ollie and I will be in the living room."

I went to the guest room and closed the door behind me. "Hi, Apple. Hi, Annie," I said, walking over to the tub.

The hamsters weren't running on the wheel. They weren't racing through the tunnel. I couldn't see them in Hannah's little house or on my stage, either.

My stomach felt wobbly. So did my head.

They must've buried themselves in the litter. I stuck my hand in. I felt along the bottom of the tub.

No hamsters.

Oh no! What would Joss do if I lost Apple and Annie? Would she stop letting us foster? My hands got sweaty as I crawled on the floor to look for them.

"Dad!" I called. "Come quick!"

"What's wrong?" he asked, hurrying into the room.

"I can't find Apple and Annie! They aren't in their tub!" I chewed my bottom lip, trying not to cry.

Dad got down next to me. "It's OK, Kaita," he said. "Hamsters are great escape artists. They're good at getting out of their cages. As the door was closed, they must be in this room somewhere."

"Annie got out yesterday," I said. "I didn't say anything because I didn't think it would happen again."

"We'll find them," Dad said.

I looked under the futon. Dad looked behind his desk. I peeked in the rubbish bin. Dad moved the stacks of paper on the floor.

"Wait," I said. "Can you hear that?"

We stood still.

"It sounds like scratching, from behind the bookcase," I said.

Dad carefully moved the bookcase away from the wall. He smiled. "Here they are!" he said.

I crawled over to look. Apple and Annie were calmly chewing on the wood. They looked really happy.

Dad picked up Apple. I picked up Annie.

"I'm so happy to see you both," I said.

I kissed the sisters on their tiny heads. Then Dad and I put them back in the tub.

"How do you think they got out?" Dad asked.

I looked at the new toys that Hannah and I had made. My stage was tall. It sat against the side of the tub. "I bet they hopped onto the stage and climbed out," I said.

"I think you're right," Dad said.

I frowned. "I suppose I should take the stage out," I said.

"I have a better idea," Dad said. "Take it out for now. When I've finished, you can put it back in."

"Can I help you?" I asked.

"Of course!" Dad said.

# CHAPTER 5

# Another long wait

Dad and I drove to the DIY shop. We bought wood, nails and a wire screen. Back at home Dad measured, cut and hammered. I didn't get to help much, but I liked to watch Dad work. Before he'd finished, I'd worked out what he was making.

"You're making a top for the tub!" I said.

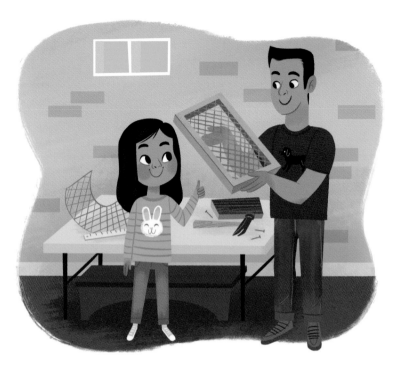

"Good guess!" Dad said. He held
up the cover. The wooden frame had
a screen to let in air and light. "Let's
try this out."

The cover fitted perfectly! I put my
stage back inside the tub. Apple and
Annie were safe in their home, and
all of us were very happy about that.

I played with the hamsters every day, as much as I could. Days went by. Weeks went by. No one came to adopt Apple and Annie.

"It can be difficult to adopt out hamsters," Mum said to me after talking to Joss. "We have to be patient and keep trying."

I liked having Apple and Annie living with us. I loved playing with them. I didn't mind cleaning their tub. It was easy. Hannah loved to come over and help, too. But I really wanted our foster animals to find their forever home.

One day I had an idea. Hannah and I had just finished playing with the hamsters.

"What if we made posters of Apple and Annie?" I asked. "We could put them up at school and in the library."

"That's a great idea," Hannah said.

We went to my room and got my art supplies. We made a pile of colourful posters. Hannah wrote the words. I drew the pictures.

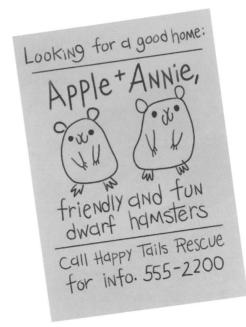

Mum drove us to our school and the library. She even let us put up a poster at her bookshop.

Two days went by. Three days went by. Finally on the fourth day, Joss called.

Mum hung up the phone and smiled. "Good news, Kaita!" she said. "A family will be coming over in a bit to meet Apple and Annie. There are two boys. One is your age. One is a bit older. And they have had a hamster before."

"Cool!" I said.

I raced to the front window and waited. Every time a car drove onto our road, I hoped it would turn into our driveway. It never did. Waiting was painful!

Then I remembered what Mum had said. If I kept busy, time would seem to pass more quickly. I grabbed a new puzzle off the shelf. This one was a picture of cartoon super heroes.

I placed the puzzle pieces onto the coffee table. Ollie curled up next to me. One by one I sorted all the edge pieces. Before I could start clicking them together, the doorbell rang.

*Yip! Yip! Yip!* Ollie ran to the door. Dad, Mum and I did, too.

"Hello!" Dad said, greeting a woman and two boys. "You must be here to see the hamsters."

"Yes, I'm Jill. These are my sons, Ethan and Harry," the woman said.

"Where are the hamsters?" Ethan, the older boy, asked.

"I'll show you," I said.

The boys followed me to the guest room. Dad carried Ollie. Mum and Jill came last. It was like a parade!

Mum took the cover off the tub, and Ethan put his hand inside. Apple came straight over. She sat still as he lifted her up and held her. Harry reached in next and picked up Annie. Both boys were very careful.

I held my breath. I hoped they would want to adopt the hamsters. Ethan stroked Apple's head with a finger. Harry told Annie how cute she was.

The boys looked at their mum.

"Can we take them home, Mum?" Ethan asked.

Jill smiled. "Yes, I think they'll be the perfect fit for our family," she said.

Hooray! Apple and Annie had found their forever home. They had waited a long time for it.

Although I was excited about our next foster pet, I could wait. I was learning how to be much better about waiting. Another foster pet would come soon enough!

# Think about it!

1. It's hard for Kaita to wait. What does she do to help pass the time? What are some things you do when you're finding it hard to wait?

2. What would you do if you were Kaita and found Annie outside her cage the first time?

3. What do Kaita and Hannah like to do when they are together? What do you like to do with your friends?

# Draw it! Write it!

1. Make a poster for Apple and Annie to try to find them a forever home. Use words and pictures to get people excited about the idea of adopting them.

2. Pretend you are Kaita and write a letter to Ethan and Harry. What would you tell them about Apple and Annie? What tips would you give them?

# Glossary

**adopt**  to take and raise as one's own

**bonded**  having a close relationship

**dachshund**  a type of dog with a long body and short legs

**dwarf hamster**  a tiny, very active rodent with a short tail

**foster**  to give care and a safe home for a short time

**fragile**  easily broken or damaged

**nocturnal**  active at night and resting during the day

**patient**  calm during difficult times

# Author talk with the real Kaita

Kaita Takano is a made-up character in this story. There is also a real Kaita. Although they share the same first name and a love for fostering pets (and both have a mini dachshund called Ollie) they have some differences. Kaita in the story is 8 years old. She's Japanese American. Real Kaita is 10 years old and is half Korean American, half European American.

Debbi Michiko Florence: Kaita, how did you get into fostering?

Kaita: My mum works with other people who foster. She overheard them talking about needing a cat foster and volunteered.

DMF: What was the first pet you fostered?

K: Our first pet was a black cat called Boo. He had a disease called cerebellar hypoplasia. He fell down a lot. I don't remember him much, though, as I was only six. To me, the most memorable pets were the mum cat and her five week-old kittens that we fostered. The mum's name was Sweetie, and the kittens were called Sprinkle, Frosting, Creamsicle, Butterscotch and Chip. Ollie thought he was their fairy dogfather!

DMF: What do you like best about fostering animals?

K: That we get to bring in pets who have been abandoned or don't have homes. We get to give them new homes with families who will love them forever.

DMF: What is the biggest challenge?

K: Sometimes the animals get poorly, and we can't help them. Other times they stay with us for a long time, and I feel bad because it seems like nobody wants them. But if you wait long enough, the right person will always come along!

DMF: What is your favourite pet that you have fostered?

K: Once we fostered two kittens called Sven and Olaf. They were fluffy white babies who loved to snuggle. They were adopted together, which was even better.

DMF: Do you have a special story you'd like to share?

K: Our pony, Angus, came from a place where they didn't take care of their ponies. A friend saved him and fixed his feet, and he came to live with us! It took a long time for him to trust grown-ups, but he liked me straight away!

DMF: Do you ever wish you could keep any of the foster pets?

K: All of them!

DMF: Why do you foster instead of keeping the pets?

K: We have kept some, but Dad says we can't keep any more! Fostering is such an easy thing to do. What's one more pet when you already have two? When the animals are in a home instead of a shelter, we can learn more about their personalities before they go to their forever families.

DMF: Is there a pet you haven't fostered yet that you'd like to?

K: Chinchillas! There were some earlier this year for adoption, but my mum said no. (Ollie said yes!)

# About the author

**Debbi Michiko Florence** writes books for children
in her writing studio, The Word Nest. She is an
animal lover with a degree in zoology and has
worked at a pet shop, the Humane Society, a raptor
rehabilitation centre and a zoo. She is the author
of two chapter book series: Jasmine Toguchi and
Dorothy & Toto. Debbi lives in Connecticut, USA,
with her husband, a rescue dog, a rabbit and
two ducks.

# About the illustrator

**Melanie Demmer** is an illustrator and designer based in Los Angeles, USA. She has created artwork for various clothing, animation and publishing projects. When she isn't making art, Melanie enjoys writing, spending time in the great outdoors, iced tea, scary films and taking naps with her cat, Pepper.

# Go on all four fun, furry foster adventures!

Apple and Annie, the Hamster Duo

Betty the Bearded Dragon

Buttons the Kitten

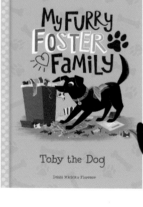

Toby the Dog

# Only from Raintree!